In Trouble with **Susie Soapsuds**

For Katie
R.I.

For Matilda
M.W.

Reading Consultant: Prue Goodwin, Lecturer in literacy and children's books

ORCHARD BOOKS
338 Euston Road, London NW1 3BH
Orchard Books Australia
Hachette Children's Books
Level 17/207 Kent Street, Sydney NSW 2000

First published in 2011 by Orchard Books
Text © Rose Impey 2011
Illustrations © Melanie Williamson 2011

ISBN 978 1 40830 222 4 (hardback)
ISBN 978 1 40830 230 9 (paperback)

1 3 5 7 9 10 8 6 4 2 (hardback)
1 3 5 7 9 10 8 6 4 2 (paperback)

Printed in China

Orchard Books is a division of Hachette Children's Books,
an Hachette UK company.

www.hachette.co.uk

In Trouble with Susie Soapsuds

Written by ROSE IMPEY

Illustrated by MELANIE WILLIAMSON

ORCHARD BOOKS

As well as always being in trouble,
Nipper McFee was always broke.

This time it was because those rotten basement rats had stolen his pocket money.

Next week was the Annual Firework Display. Nipper's friends, Will and Lil, had already bought their tickets.

The fountains would fizz, the
rockets would race into the air and
the bangers would . . . *bang*!
But Nipper would miss it all.

"I need a plan," Nipper told Will and Lil. "A get-rich-quick plan."

"Uh oh," thought Lil. Nipper had tried a few of those plans in the past and they always ended in trouble.

"Remember the lizard!" she said.

One time Nipper had tried to earn some money by walking the neighbours' pets.

He'd walked Mrs Lulu Lamb's lizard – but somehow he'd lost it.

It hadn't been Nipper's fault . . .
but Nipper got the blame.

"And remember the milk float,"
said Will.

That time Mr Mewler had let Nipper deliver the milk.

Thanks to the rats, the milk float
went floating down the canal.
And Nipper got the blame again.

This time Nipper needed a
trouble-free plan.

"What about a pavement sale?"
said Lil.

Nipper went home and collected
a bagful of toys.

It might have been trouble-free – if his mum hadn't walked by just then.

She soon spotted his sisters' favourite dolls. And his brother Monty's saxophone.
Nipper was in trouble – again.

Now it was only two days until the firework display. Nipper was desperate.

He found Will and Lil in the laundrette, collecting their family wash.

It was very busy. Everyone wanted their washing done.

Poor Susie Soapsuds was almost run off her feet. She hadn't had a break all day. "If only I had someone to help me," she said.

This was Nipper's chance.

Susie Soapsuds went off for her lunch, leaving Nipper in charge. He thought, "This will be easy-peasy."

Nipper took out his comic and
put up his feet.
He started reading all about his
hero, Crazy Cat.

So Nipper didn't see those sneaky
basement rats walk by – but the
rats saw *him*.
They were looking for trouble, as
usual. Now they had found it.

They mixed up the loads of washing,

they turned up
the temperatures . . .

and turned down
the fans.

Soon the place was full of steam.
Nipper couldn't even see his comic.
So he didn't see those rotten rodents
sneaking out of the door.

When Susie Soapsuds came back,
she couldn't believe her eyes.

All the clothes had shrunk . . .

or changed colour . . .

or looked as if their
owners had slept
in them.

When Nipper realised what had happened, he said, "OK. Now it's war!"

Nipper raced home and borrowed
his mother's laundry basket.

He laid a trap for his pesky enemies
and the stupid rats walked straight
into it.

The next time Susie Soapsuds took a break, Nipper and his friends sneaked in.

They gave those basement rats the best
scrubbing they'd ever had – followed
by a quick dip in the dye tub.
Then Nipper collected back his
pocket money.

As the fountains fizzed and the rockets raced into the air, Nipper stopped to think about his rotten enemies still hanging out to dry.

"It was all fair and square," he thought. "And anyway, it was time those rats learned the price of messing with Nipper."

ROSE IMPEY   MELANIE WILLIAMSON

All priced at £8.99

Orchard Books are available from all good bookshops,
or can be ordered from our website: www.orchardbooks.co.uk,
or telephone 01235 827702, or fax 01235 827703.

Prices and availability are subject to change.

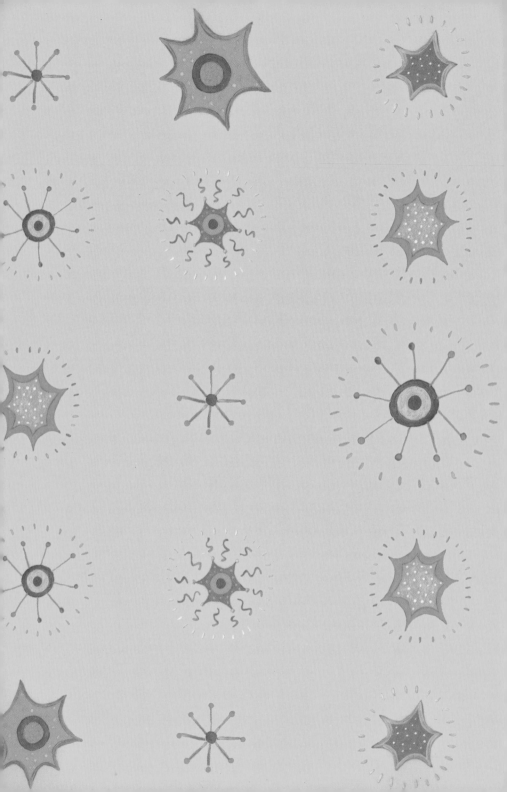